MY NAME IS HAMBURGER

MY NAME IS HAMBURGER

JACQUELINE JULES

KAR-BEN PUBLISHING

KAR-BEN PUBLISHING®
An imprint of Lerner Publishing Group, Inc.
241 First Avenue North
Minneapolis, MN 55401 USA

Website address: www.karben.com

Jacket illustration by Mira Miroslavova.

Patterned background by Siu-Hong Mok/Shutterstock.com.

Main body text set in Bembo Std.
Typeface provided by Monotype Typography

Library of Congress Cataloging-in-Publication Data

Names: Jules, Jacqueline, 1956- author.
Title: My name is Hamburger / by Jacqueline Jules.
Description: Minneapolis : Kar-Ben Publishing, an imprint of Lerner Publishing Group, Inc., [2022] | Audience: Ages 8–13. | Audience: Grades 4–6. | Summary: Told in verse, fourth grader Trudie Hamburger feels out of place in 1962 America due to her immigrant father and Jewish identity, until a new classmate and an accident help her embrace her differences.
Identifiers: LCCN 2021033554 | ISBN 9781728429489 | ISBN 9781728429496 (paperback)
Subjects: CYAC: Novels in verse. | Jews—United States—Fiction. | Bullying—Fiction. | Family life—Fiction. | Friendship—Fiction.
Classification: LCC PZ7.5.J85 My 2022 | DDC [Fic]—dc23

LC record available at https://lccn.loc.gov/202103355454

Manufactured in the United States of America
1-49451-49517-12/23/2021

In loving memory of my father, Otto

Rainy Afternoon, March 1962

The best place to spend a rainy afternoon
is Lila's basement, in the house beside mine,
swaying on her checkerboard floor,
singing along with Brenda Lee.

Lila likes the fast songs.
I like the slow ones, to feel
the shiver of each note
floating from the record player.

Lila's wearing a blue collared dress
with short, puffy sleeves. Her ponytail
tied up in a matching bow.

She says next time, I shouldn't come
still dressed for school, in a brown sweater
and plaid skirt. I should wear something nice
for pretending we're on TV.

We both dream of singing on Ed Sullivan's
Sunday night show, of being Brenda Lee,

who's only 4 foot 9 and gives us hope
that someone small can still be famous.

They've called her Little Miss Dynamite
since she was twelve, two years older
than Lila and me.

I'd love a nickname like that,
one I could be proud of.

I'd love to open my mouth one day
and show the world my big, beautiful sound.

But right now, I am happy just to be
dancing in my best friend's basement, believing
all my dreams will come true.

Two Babies on a Blanket

I met Lila when I was six months old,
not that I really remember, of course.

Momma says we were two babies on a blanket,
bows on bald heads, staring at each other.

Mrs. Cummings, Lila's momma, likes
to have coffee and cookies with mine.

"So cute, the way you two grew up together,"
Mrs. Cummings often says. "Side by side."

In houses, maybe—not in height. Lila's been smaller
than me, smaller than everybody our age,
since we took our first steps
in her mother's lemon-yellow kitchen.

That hasn't stopped Lila from
taking the lead. She's the baby of three girls
and has learned to speak up fast, before all the best
chocolates are gone from the box.

Unlike me, who usually waits, lets others pick first,
gets stuck with the leftovers no one else wants.

I don't like fights I can't win. I know better
than to argue with Lila, to choose *Monopoly*
when she wants to play *Concentration*.
That's why, when we're done singing
Mrs. Cummings is surprised
to find me still in her house.

"I didn't hear your voice, Trudie," she says.
"Only Lila's."

Spelling Bee News

Daddy comes home from his print shop at six,
the time I'm supposed to leave Lila's
and be home for dinner. I run through the raindrops
across her yard and mine, up the steps to our porch,
to find Daddy already there, waiting to hug me.

"How was school?" he wants to know,
like he always does, and I tell him "Fine,"
like I always do, even though it's rarely true.

Except today, I have extra news for Daddy.
My spelling test: 100 percent four weeks
in a row. It means Mrs. Bryan chose me
to represent our fourth-grade class
in the schoolwide bee,
coming this Friday.

"My daughter!" Daddy grins.
"The American!"

Daddy says kids in Germany,
where he grew up, didn't have contests
to learn how to spell.

"It's for English," he tells me, "because
so many words don't follow rules."

Daddy knows firsthand
there's a lot to memorize.
And he's helping me learn
every night with his red dictionary,
the one he used to teach himself
how to read and write
for a new life in America.

Hamburger

When I walk into the kitchen,
I can smell that Momma's broiling
hamburgers, the way our family likes,
with onion soup mix inside.

It's one of our favorite meals.
All for different reasons.

Momma likes how my baby brother
puts the soft chopped meat into his mouth,
not all over his high chair tray or on his head.

Daddy says he loves hamburgers because he ate them
for the first time at a barbecue, before he was married,
when he was learning to love American things,
including my mother.

I like how my family sits at our round table
just eating a tasty food, not a last name
I wish didn't go with my first.

At home, I'm just a girl enjoying
dinner, not the Trudie Hamburger
kids tease at school.

Daniel Reynolds

He squints his dark eyes,
which makes him look mean
before he ever opens his mouth.

And he thinks a Jewish girl
with the last name Hamburger
deserves that cackly laugh
I hear each time he looks my way.

Sitting beside him in Mrs. Bryan's class,
I can see the red marks on his papers.

Daniel Reynolds never came close
to qualifying for the spelling bee.

Not that it matters to any of the boys
who join him on the playground
to call me "chopped meat."

But Mrs. Bryan seems to care.
This happy morning, she's decided

Daniel should move his desk
closer to the blackboard, closer
to the words he writes down wrong.

For the first time since September,
I'm not stiff in my seat by the window,
careful not to move my eyes too far
to the right. I can look straight
across the aisle at Lila and wave
if I want to—even wink.

The Spelling List

Before we leave for the day,
Mrs. Bryan hands me a list:
words I can practice
for the spelling bee.

I see "mournful" and "melancholy,"
"potent" and "powerful."

"Just do your best," Mrs. Bryan says,
"And use the microphone."

The tone of her voice tells me
she doesn't think I will last
on the stage too long.
Sixth graders always win.

Mrs. Bryan doesn't know
how many nights I've studied
with Daddy, how I already
know all those words on her list,

and how winning means
more than beating sixth graders.
It means Daniel Reynolds
will be sorry he made a fool of himself,
laughing at the fourth-grade girl
who won the spelling bee.

Sue Ellen

Lila grabs my hand and swings it high
like a shopping bag on a spending spree.

We're both excited. Me for the spelling bee
coming at the end of the week. Lila because
Sue Ellen Bridges walked partway
home with us. First time!

Sue Ellen agreed, at Lila's urging,
to take Acorn instead of Abbott.

Hardly a detour, Lila explained,
since Sue Ellen's big Colonial
with the tall white columns
sits right in the middle of West,
a half block either way.

Sue Ellen has long brown curls
and a face to match the pretty pastel
dresses she wears every day of the week.

My mother buys me more practical
clothes for school—no tiny buttons,
ruffles, or lace to repair.

Lila's mother does the same.
Maybe that's why Lila follows
Sue Ellen with puppy-dog eyes
begging for a biscuit treat.

Or maybe it's because Lila got
invited to Sue Ellen's birthday
at the Colburn Country Club,
where Jewish girls like me
are not allowed.

Lila said the party was too grown-up.
Everyone sitting primly, trying not to spill
in the fancy dining room with white tablecloths.

But it didn't make me feel better
that I couldn't go.

Spelling Bee Stage

Friday is finally here,
and I'm on the school stage
waiting my turn, my right hand
tugging my hem, trying to cover
the Band-Aid on my knee.

Row after row of faces, watching me,
can see I tripped on the blacktop.

Just like they'll hear if I miss my next word.

So far, I've been lucky. The judge's cruel bell
hasn't dinged at "homogenous,"
"honorable," or the other long words
I spoke loud and clear, the microphone
taking my voice to the very back of the room.

So far I've been B-R-I-L-L-I-A-N-T,
sparkling with bright luster—the definition
of my dreams when I am alone in bed,
seeing stars through the ceiling.

There are only two of us left standing
between the heavy red curtains. Only two.
Kemper Watson and me. Caroline Baldwin
just heard the bell. She ran down the side stairs,
hands on her eyes, sent out for forgetting one
of the "p's" in D-I-S-A-P-P-O-I-N-T-E-D.

Not me. Not yet. I still have
a chance to hear my name and "winner"
in the same sentence, said out loud.

No more Trudie Hamburger, the girl
who cries when Daniel Reynolds teases.

In her place, a smiling girl
who holds a gold trophy for the newspaper
and never falls on the playground again.

Silent H

The judge gives me
a short word. Only
two syllables.

An easy word.
Should spell the way it sounds
and make all the hands
in this big room with its rows
and rows of fold-down seats
clap, clap, clap for me.

Ready to win,
I open my mouth
at the microphone.
No sigh or
deep breath first.

R-Y-T-H-M.

Ding! Ding!

The bell is as shrill as a whistle,
screeching the *H* that the judge says
belongs before the *Y*
in *R-H-Y-T-H-M.*

I missed the silent *H.*

Like in gherkin.
That little green pickle
kids like to crunch.

Off the Stage

The shiny wood seat open beside Lila
is five spots down from Daniel Reynolds,
who's snarling at the end of the aisle.

"LOSER!" His growl should have warned
me to pick another row, to keep my distance.
But I wanted to sit between Lila
and Sue Ellen Bridges, not alone in the back
with no one to pat my knee, tell me next year
would come with another chance.

"You missed an easy word!"

His shoes strike my ankles like a fist,
punching me as I squeeze past.
My eyes sting.

"I thought Jews were smart," he says.

Consolation Prize

Sue Ellen flips a long brown curl
over her shoulder as I plop down,
finally safe from Daniel's shoes.

"Second place!" she says. "Wow!"

What? Could it be? Praise
from Sue Ellen Bridges?

"Five rounds in the final," Sue Ellen says.
"No fourth grader's ever gone that far."

Lila's beaming, her head bobbing,
so pleased I caught Sue Ellen's eye.

"We were holding hands," Lila says.
"Wishing for you with all our might!"

“Mrs. Bryan was excited too,” Sue Ellen adds.
“She was biting her nails.”

Sue Ellen’s nod and smile.
Not the spelling trophy I wanted,
but a consolation prize.

Red Ribbon Pictures

Kemper Watson hugs
his gold cup trophy for the camera.
It's bigger than the space I made
on my bedroom dresser, just in case.

My eyes make note while the man
in the striped tie from the *Colburn News*
remembers how last year Kemper
held my red ribbon.

"Tried again," he writes on his spiral pad
with a ballpoint pen. "Good for you."

He poses me with my red ribbon
and Caroline Baldwin with her white ribbon
on either side of Kemper for the morning edition
Daddy always reads first thing with eggs and coffee.

The flashbulb makes me see spots
and a vision of next year,
when I stand in the middle
holding the big gold cup
against my grinning cheek.

Popsicles

After pictures,
I move through the green halls to Room 12,
my mind seeing Daddy's gold-capped tooth
gleaming with the news his daughter's face
will be in the morning paper.

I don't expect anything better from this day
that has already pitched me back and forth
like my baby brother's rocking horse.

When I walk through the doorway,
the sound of clapping hands startles me.
GOOD JOB, TRUDIE! shines in
white cursive letters from the blackboard.

Mrs. Bryan is so proud
of the girl who represented her class
and made it all the way to second place,
she takes us outside with a box of popsicles.

I get to be first in line.

With frozen rainbow on my tongue,
the ding of the bell onstage
and the bite of Daniel Reynolds's shoes
don't taste quite as bitter as before.

Bellwood Court

After school, Sue Ellen walks with us
again. We wave goodbye at the corner
and continue down Acorn Street,
under long, empty branches
waiting to sprout spring leaves.

Acorn ends in a turn to the right
and a circle called Bellwood Court.
It has three houses: Mine, Lila's,
and Jerry Braswell's. His family
moved here from Lovettsville
last summer.

In June, we gave Jerry
the clothespin and card
he clipped to his spokes
so his bike could sound
like a motorcycle
zooming down the street.

We waved at his silhouette
behind gauzy curtains, a signal
to come down to the creek
for a game of tag.

In July, Jerry skipped over the sprinkler
and danced with us by Daddy's roses.
He shook out his shaggy red hair
like an Irish setter in the rain.

But in August, Jerry Braswell left
Bellwood Court for three weeks.
Boy Scout Camp with Daniel Reynolds,
where he learned boys shouldn't splash
and giggle with girls by the roses.
They should snicker and snort
whenever a girl comes near.

SPLAT!

When we reach
our blacktop circle,
we hear the sound
of stifled laughter.

Lila's neck swivels
faster than an owl's head.

We see Jerry Braswell's red hair
peeking up through the tall bushes
that line his front lawn like a fence.
Another head bobs beside him.
A dark-haired one.

Cackling, high and sharp,
echoes across the asphalt.

"That sounds like Daniel Reynolds."
Lila drops her schoolbag to step closer.

Lila can't see how small she looks
tiptoeing across Bellwood Court,
the shortest girl in our class. Yet inside,
she is so much taller than me, timid
as an owlet hopping two feet behind her.

We see something round and red
sail into the street. *SPLAT!*
It lands by Lila's saddle shoe.

Water balloons! Coming as fast
as snowballs in a fight where
only one side has ammunition.

We fly off like birds with wet feathers,
our feelings soaked.

Nothing Broken

We rush into my house
so fast, the screen door slams
and Momma warns,
"You'll wake Sammy!"

My brother's nap always comes first,
making Mrs. Cummings, visiting
for coffee, the one to comfort
two girls in the kitchen,
gasping over dripping skirts.

"What happened, honey?" Lila's mom,
not mine, touches shoulders
and checks for bruises. My momma leans
her long, thin back against the counter,
right fist on pale lips, silent
as my sleeping brother upstairs,
while Mrs. Cummings explains
in a breezy voice how a neighbor
friend turned traitor isn't the crime
we think it to be.

"Water bombs are just silly boys playing."

"No one's hurt." Momma finally speaks.
"Nothing broken."

Only red balloons, scattered
in little pieces all over the street
along with my trust
in mothers who understand.

Sammy's Big Sister

Mrs. Cummings takes Lila's hand
to leave Momma and me in the kitchen
alone with the news I still haven't shared.
Second place in the spelling bee.
My picture coming in the morning paper.

Noises, like a mewling cat,
shut my mouth before it opens.

Momma rushes upstairs
to my little brother's room.

Since the November day
Sammy was born—a month early—
my mother's ears
have only heard his cries.

In this house, I am Sammy's big sister,
the child Momma tells to be patient
when two-year-old fingers rip my magazine,
toss the socks from my drawers.

Sammy's big sister. The child
who doesn't need "constant watching."

I don't climb over the couch,
pull cords from the counter,
grab glasses off the table.

And I don't cry in a crib
with my little arms raised,
waiting to be picked up
and covered with the kisses
that all belong to Sammy now.

Green Porch Swing

It's Friday afternoon,
an hour before sundown.

I am waiting
on the green cushions
of our porch swing, listening
to its chirpy creak.

Any time now,
Daddy's white van
will chug past our house,
down the long driveway
to the old barn garage
where Daddy keeps
his gardening tools.

When he cuts off the engine,
I won't jump up to shout my news
before he can step one brown shoe
down from the tall driver's seat.

I'll stay where I am, pretending
to read the new biography
Daddy will ask to see
when he sits down
on the creaky green swing
for our end-of-the-day chat.

Daddy always likes to hear
about Annie Oakley and
Molly Pitcher and anyone else
who was special enough
to end up in my library books.

But the swing will creak
with a different tune today
when I wave a red ribbon
and drop it smack
in Daddy's lap.

Wunderkind

"My little girl is a star!"

Daddy shows off the gold tooth
I see best when he smiles.

"*Wunderkind!*" He tickles my ears
with the German word
he saves for when he's extra proud.

Daddy calls himself a New American.
That means he's still learning American things.
Like the rules in baseball and Halloween.
Could it be that Daddy doesn't know
a red ribbon means second place, not first?

Should I let him go on
calling me *wunderkind*
and whiz kid? Or correct him
in a gentle voice,
the way Momma does

when he says
an English word wrong?

There's no bell ringing, saying
I have to get off the stage.

Why can't I stay
on the porch swing just a little longer,
gleaming in the evening sun,
just like Daddy's gold-toothed smile?

Friday Night

In the dining room,
candles glow on tall stands
like a scene from a fairy-tale castle.

Red roses bloom on Momma's china
and on her cheeks. Daddy smiles
as she sets the last dish on the table.
Noodle kugel with raisins and apples.

Even Sammy is quiet in his high chair,
watching Daddy lift a silver cup
to sing Kiddush.

He knows there's grape juice
when the song is over,
and he waits with big brown eyes,
looking sweet, like the baby brother
I wanted when Momma first
told me he was coming.

On Friday night, my family feels
braided like the challah bread
Momma baked in the morning.

We belong at this table, together,
eating a bread blessed by a Hebrew prayer
no one else at my school understands.

The walls flicker with candlelight.

We're in a castle protected by a moat
no enemies can cross.

Jewish Church

Lila pouts the next morning
when she sees me in the driveway
dressed in purple velveteen
and patent leather shoes.

She complains that I'm always gone
on Saturdays until the afternoon,
when my family gets home
from Beth Israel Congregation,
thirty miles from Colburn.

"Why do you go to that Jewish church?"
she asks. "You should come with me
on Sundays. New Hope Baptist is close,
only four blocks from Bellwood Court."

It's true that services
on Sundays would bring me closer
to her and everyone else in Colburn.

But it would take me away
from the Saturday mornings I've known
since I was Sammy's age, hearing
Rabbi Hertz chant the Torah, his voice rising
and falling like a wave on the ocean.

At Beth Israel, something inside me
floats, singing songs I know so well.
My lips move all on their own.

I wave at Lila
from the station wagon window,
wondering if she'll ever understand
how a place miles from where I live
can be where I feel most at home.

Our Space

At Beth Israel, there is a nice woman
who watches Sammy and two other little boys
in a playroom while Momma and Daddy
take me upstairs to the sanctuary.

We sit in the middle, five rows from the front,
on the left side. Our space in the sanctuary—
as if a teacher wrote our name on the seats.

Even when we come a little late because
traffic is slow, our row is waiting for us.
Rabbi Hertz smiles and nods
as we open our prayer books
behind the Kaplan family and in front
of Mr. and Mrs. Rosenstein. Our friends
the Feldmans sit across the way.

I settle in my seat on the aisle
and wave at Dina, who pats her tummy,
already hungry for the lunch
we'll eat later in the social hall.

Kids Like Me

Dina doesn't like lox. She eats her bagel
with cream cheese only. No tomato or purple onion
either. We are the same. Except she goes to school
with the Bloom brothers, the Cohen sisters,
Julie Geller, and Sid Gold. Dina sees kids
who celebrate Hanukkah, not Christmas,
in the cafeteria or the playground all week.
I only see kids like me on Saturdays, after Daddy drives
thirty miles in a blue station wagon with wood trim.

Dina tells me it's hard for her too.
"There aren't many of us at school,"
she says. "Last week, a boy asked me
to take off my shoe, to see if
my foot was human or devil." She whispers
this in our corner, where we picnic,
napkins spread on the floor,
lemonade cups beside our paper plates.
I chew my bagel and wonder what
I would do if Daniel Reynolds questioned
the toes inside my shoes.

Daniel already has enough to say
about my name and what he calls my "Jewish nose."

"I showed that boy," Dina says with a wink.

"Really?" I ask, blinking.

"Yep!" She smiles. "And I threw my stinky sock
in his face!"

Fair Lakes Nursery

On Sunday, it's sunny.
Daddy and I stand by the picture window
after breakfast, plotting.

"What do you think?" he asks.
"Do we need more roses?"

It's not really a question. Daddy's
already reaching for his plaid cap.
I'm already putting on my jacket.
We wave goodbye to Momma
and head for Daddy's van,
the one that says "Colburn Printing"
and has enough room in the back
for new bushes to come home.

A trip to Fair Lakes Nursery means
spring is coming as surely as the crocus
peeking purple heads through the mulch.

As we park the van, Mr. Pritchard
comes to the gate, ready to show us
bare root roses unloaded from the truck
just yesterday. "Don't stop there," Daddy urges.
"Show me all your new arrivals."

We stroll through the aisles of pots and petals
till lunchtime. Daddy and Mr. Pritchard yakking on
about the best time to plant this or that
and if a new fertilizer is worth a try.

Mr. Pritchard understands Daddy's every word.
No pauses or puzzled looks—like when Daddy speaks
to Lila's dad or the cashier at the A & P.

My daddy, talking the language of flowers,
on a morning as pretty as the primroses
with their yellow eyes and purple faces.

Bare Root Roses

Daddy doesn't have to explain
so much to me anymore.
I know that the hole has to be bigger
than the roots. That a bare plant
will grow fast and strong,
giving us bright blooms later.

I like using the big fork
to break up the soil
and mix in the peat moss.

And watching Daddy,
how careful he is,
putting the plant
in the hole just right.
How he pats the dirt down
in a mound like he's making
a sandcastle. How he lets me
use the watering can first.

Daddy doesn't see
green branches sticking
up from the ground.
He doesn't see thorns.

His brown eyes glow
with what he promises I'll see
in just ten or twelve weeks, before
school is out for the summer.

A bush blooming with roses
as yellow and bright
as the March sun in the sky.

Monday Music

Monday is music day for everyone
in Mrs. Bryan's class except me.
I go to the library to sit with Mrs. Nolan.
Except I don't sit. She's taught me
how to shelve *A* to *Z*. So I am
busy putting books in the right places.
Sometimes I find a book out of order
or upside down. Mrs. Nolan is always happy
to hear I've rescued it, put it where it belongs.

Sort of like me, who doesn't belong in music
with the rest of my class, not this year
with the new music teacher, Mrs. Thompson.

She has two jobs. One at Pine Hill Elementary
and the other at New Hope Baptist,
where she runs the Sunday choir.

Mrs. Thompson didn't like seeing
my head bent and my lips closed

for the Christmas songs she brought
from her church, celebrating Jesus.

Momma had to come to school for a meeting
with Mr. Preston in the principal's office,
where the grown-ups all agreed.
Mrs. Thompson shouldn't have to change
her choice of sacred music for just one child.

"Trudie might feel more comfortable
in the library," Mrs. Thompson said
as Mr. Preston nodded.

Momma blinked, but in her eyes
I could see her belief
that Jewish people
shouldn't make waves.

She told Mrs. Thompson, "Yes,
my Trudie loves books."

And Momma's right. I do love books.
Just about as much as I love to sing.

Piano Lessons

Thursday afternoons, I walk to Mrs. Cartwright's house
with the music books I should have opened more.

Mrs. Cartwright has a bent back and a wispy, white bun,
but she's kind and doesn't complain too much about
my slow fingers slipping on her black-and-white keys.

She knows my favorite part of our hour together
comes at the end, when she plays for me. Today,
we sing "Follow the Yellow Brick Road"
and "Over the Rainbow" from *The Wizard of Oz*.

When my lips open beside Mrs. Cartwright's
baby grand, the sound swirls over the shiny, black wood
like it's coming from a crystal bell, making me believe
I could fly over the rainbow and onto a stage
where thousands of people listen to me.

Mrs. Cartwright claps, calling me the best part
of her lonely week. She wants to know
why she hasn't heard me at school concerts.

"The music teacher should give you a solo."

I lower my eyes with a "thank you,"
knowing it wouldn't be wise
to say Mrs. Thompson asked me
to leave her class at Christmastime
without an invitation to return.

Mrs. Cartwright might not even know
I don't celebrate the same holidays
as everyone else in Colburn. In December,
she gave me an angel on a string.

"Because you sound like one," she said,
holding my hands in hers.

Reading Race

Since I go to the library twice a week, once
during music and once with my class,
I have extra time to get books, extra time
for reading. And it shows in the sky-blue
reading chart hanging just to the left
of our classroom door. The gold stars
beside my name are moving closer
and closer to the finish line.

The first to read fifty books wins the trophy
on Mrs. Bryan's desk. It's not as big as the one
Kemper Watson held for winning the spelling bee,
but I'm still hungry for the chance to bring it home.

In Lila's house, a dozen gold figures shine
on the fireplace mantel. Her daddy's bowling team
wins every year, and Lila loves to show me
the newest one, so tall it reaches her waist.

Will I ever have a shiny prize? To put on display.
Something declaring that I won. That once,
I was the best.

As we line up to leave, I lift my finger to count
my reading stars, the way I always do.
Today, Sue Ellen stops me.

"No need to check, Trudie," she says,
swatting my hand down. "All that time
you spend in the library. Of course
you have the advantage."

With a shake of her long curls, Sue Ellen
glides past me as if my stars were stolen
from her and everybody else who's welcome
in music on Mondays.

Don't Cry

Lila is kind on the walk home,
her arm around my shoulder,
a fresh hankie pressed into my palm.

Sue Ellen has ballet today
and was picked up
in her mother's red Cadillac.

So it's safe for me to sniff a little,
say how much the reading race
matters after losing the spelling bee.

Lila says don't cry,
Sue Ellen didn't mean her words
the way they sounded to me.

"Sue Ellen's just jealous," Lila says,
"because you're so smart."

"Are you sure?" I dab my eyes,
doubting Sue Ellen's envy of me,
the girl she doesn't invite
to parties at the country club.

"Of course," Lila says. "Everybody knows
Jewish people are brainy."

Lila taps my head, hoping to make me smile.
I do what she expects, telling myself
she doesn't mean her words
the way they sound to me.

Good News

On Friday night, Daddy comes
to the Shabbos table, promising good news
after candles, Kiddush, and Motzi.

The blessings always come first, so I'm wiggling
in my chair, wanting to know what's made
Daddy grin as wide as a chipmunk trying
to hold in cheeks full of nuts.

"The blossoms have popped!" Daddy finally tells us
as Sammy chomps on challah and Momma
takes bowls to serve soup. "We should
celebrate spring."

Daddy has Sunday plans. We'll leave
early in the morning for Washington, DC,
and the famous trees blooming
by the monuments. "Trudie has only seen
them on TV," he says. "She should see
them in full color this year."

"A Sunday outing!" Momma smiles
as she sets down the soup.
"First one in ages!"

Reminding me how long it's been
since we took Sammy anywhere on Sunday,
how he runs
every which way
or cries and stamps his little feet.

"*Ja!*" Daddy nods. "A day with my family
and the flowers!"

Dreaming in Pink

Saturday night, Momma lays out
my pink dress with front pockets,
pressed and ready for Washington, DC.

"You'll match the cherry blossoms," Momma says
as she rummages the drawer for pink socks too.

I put my head on the pillow,
certain I will dream in pink all night.
My parents have promised a picnic
by the Tidal Basin, the glittering pool
that helped them fall in love.

"The monuments have memories for us," Daddy said
at dinner, taking Momma's hand in a way I hadn't seen
since Sammy was born and my parents forgot how
to hop in the car and visit the lake or the county fair.

I lie in bed, tingling for tomorrow. Thomas Jefferson
in his round dome. Abraham Lincoln in his giant chair.

Blossoms floating in the water. All I have to do
is wait till daylight to see all that Daddy described.

Except when morning comes, Sammy is crying.
He has sniffles and a fever. No trip for Sammy today.

"But what about me?" I ask. "What about me?"

Daddy and Daughter Day

Momma gathers Sammy in her arms
and sighs, eyes on Daddy. He stares back
as if they can speak without saying a word.

"Take Trudie," Momma finally says.
"Have a daddy and daughter day."

I've never heard better words
and never dressed so fast, ready to go
before anyone has second thoughts
about a special day just for me.

"Take the picnic," Momma reminds us
as I rush out the door, Daddy one step
behind me.

The cherry blossoms are waiting for us.
I can already see how pretty they will be
in my father's smile as he backs the van
down the driveway. "We're off!" he says,
reminding me of the song in *The Wizard of Oz*.

And before I know it, I'm singing
about meeting the wizard and
how wonderful he is.

Daddy joins in, his low voice
happy beneath mine, and I feel
like Dorothy, full of adventure,
following the yellow brick road.

On the Road

Daddy's delivery van is higher
than our station wagon. I bounce
in my seat, blinking at
farmers' fences and fields.

For the first hour, we see mostly
cows and grass on our side
of the yellow line. Then the road opens
and we have two lanes, then four.

More cars appear. Trucks too.
We pass under green signs
showing us which highway to take
for our day in the city.

Daddy admires the big buildings
all around. Says he likes home,
but it's nice to travel sometimes
and see what's outside
the quiet streets of Colburn
where most everyone lives

in a two-story house, not much
taller than the ladder he uses
to clean the gutters.

"You won't believe the view,"
Daddy says, "at five hundred feet
from the Washington Monument."

"A different world," he says.

One I can't wait to see.

At the Tidal Basin

A gigantic pond surrounded
by a sidewalk and more people
than I've ever seen in one place.

Most of them have cameras
to snap picture after picture
of pink branches bending
over the water, graceful
as a ballerina's arms.

We pass a bride, posing
under the blossoms
in a long lace dress
and a swirling veil.

Everyone is taking photos
except Daddy, who says
we can buy a postcard,
prettier than any picture
his Brownie camera
can make. Daddy wants to see

the flowers with his own eyes,
not behind a lens. He wants
to hang over the railing with me
and watch the water glitter
in the sun. I tell him it looks
as if the stars have dropped
from the sky and are twinkling
like Tinkerbell's wand, ready
to grant my wish.

"What is it?" Daddy asks,
eyes smiling into mine.
"What do you wish?"

My Wish

Easy. I want to stay
in this day of dancing petals,
to always be strolling
on this sidewalk, between
my father in his plaid cap
and a man in a turban.

A few steps down, a lady
is wearing a crimson sari
and no one is staring.

Not even at the bearded man
in the long black coat and yarmulke.

The crowd at the Tidal Basin
doesn't care how you dress or
what language you speak.

I belong here, beneath
the fluffy clouds of flowers
with the sunshine on the water.

"Can we stay forever?"
I ask Daddy as my wish.

Daddy shakes his head as I expect and
suggests something else, something he says
could be a souvenir of our special day,
only bigger than the postcard we bought
in the bottom of Jefferson's dome.

"A cherry tree," Daddy says. "Why don't we
plant one in our backyard?"

Pink Petals by the Creek

We visit Mr. Pritchard's nursery
the very next Sunday.
He has three trees to show us,
and I get to choose the one with
the most flowers. Twenty-five,
to be exact. Even though
it's skinny as a broomstick,
with a bottom wrapped
in burlap like a baby's diaper,
right away it feels like mine,
and I want to pick where
it will go in our backyard.

"Can we plant it by the creek?"
I ask Daddy. "So we can see
pink petals in the water?"

"Like the Tidal Basin." Daddy nods
as he unloads my tree from the van.

Of course we both know the little creek
running behind our house is no match
for the park in Washington, DC.
But it still has soft green grass
for sitting with a book
on a nice afternoon.

As Daddy picks up his shovel,
I see myself next spring,
turning pages under my tree,
a pink cloud over my head and a creek
gurgling like a love song beside me.

My Baby Tree

Daddy and I have picked a spot
close to the edge, but not too close,
so my baby tree has plenty of room
for branching out as it grows up.

"Will it last fifty years?" I ask Daddy.
"Like the ones in Washington?"

"We can hope," he says. "Trees
can live a long time with good care."

"So *my* tree will last forever," I say,
giving it a hug.

"If you water it," Daddy warns.
"A new sapling needs a good long drink."

While Daddy goes to the house
to hook up the hose, I give my baby
one more hug, just in time

for two boys to come rustling through
the woods on the other side of the stream.

Daniel Reynolds. Ruining my Sunday
with the same snarly voice
I hate at school.

"Did you see that, Jerry?" Daniel points.
"Hamburger's hugging a tree."

"Weirdo." Jerry snickers.

They are still standing there, taunting
with cupped hands, when Daddy comes up
behind me with the hose.

Go Home!

Daddy's eyes flicker like
he knows we have enemies,
but I wonder why,
since I've never told him
Daniel Reynolds calls me
"chopped meat," teases me at
every turn, and never passes up
the chance to remind me I'm Jewish.

Daddy waves his arms, the water
from the hose spraying in circles.
He faces the boys, asking why
they bother his daughter, call her names.

"Go home!" he shouts, as if he's scaring
off stray dogs. "Leave us alone!"

The boys run away like Daddy's a bear
and they are sure to get eaten. I wish I could smile,
be happy they're gone, but something inside me
worries. Daniel has heard my daddy speak
and I may never hear the end of it.

Vy! Vy! Vy!

In the lunch line on Monday,
Daniel jabbers like a magpie.

"Vy do you bohzer my Trudie?"

"Iz not nice to call names."

"Vy! Vy! Vy!"

I turn my head to the side.
Stare at the little tiles
on the cafeteria wall. They're
green like a stink bug, smudged
and chipped, but nicer to look at
than Jerry and the other boys
chanting. "Say it again! Say it again!"

"Vy! Vy! Vy!" Daniel repeats
a fourth time, a fifth, a sixth.

My question too. Why, why, why?
Why does Daddy's voice,
so dear to my ears at home, sound
foreign—even to me—everywhere else?

I'm Safer Here

Monday afternoon is better.
Mrs. Nolan greets me with a smile
and Susan B. Anthony, a new biography
she's saved just for me.

"From the series you love," Mrs. Nolan says,
her kind voice surrounding me like all
the books in this big carpeted room.

We're way past Christmas, and no one
asks anymore why I slip into the library
while the rest of my class marches on
down the hall to Mrs. Thompson.

No one misses me, no one wants me back.

Lila says they're singing Easter songs,
mostly about bunnies and bluebells,
and only one would make me lower my eyes
and stare at the floor.

I am safer here with Mrs. Nolan,
where I don't have to decide
whether I feel good or not
singing words I don't believe.

Preparing for Passover

Momma has a sponge in her hand
when I come through the door.
She's been scrubbing all day.
Every cabinet wiped clean.
No crumbs allowed on Passover,
not in Momma's kitchen,
where every nook and cranny
will be scoured and spotless.

On Passover, we rid the house
of pretzels and pasta, biscuits and bread.
For one week, cereal and toast
are forbidden. We eat flat matzah
and macaroons instead. To remember
the exodus from Egypt; the cruel Pharaoh
who made the Jews carry bricks,
forced them to live as slaves, in fear.

At Momma's request, I empty my schoolbag,
turn out my pockets, check my closet
for stale cookies and crackers.

Momma comes in with the sweeper,
and together we vacuum the floor. It takes work
to be ready for Passover, a holiday
that reminds us how hard it is to be free.

Messy Meringues

With the kitchen clean, it's time for cookies.

Momma always likes my help, rolling
balls out of batter for the baking sheet.

After the macaroons, we make meringues.

Momma teaches me to beat the egg whites
till they're stiff, add the sugar and the chocolate,
just like her mother, my bubbe, taught her.

I feel tall this year, standing on a step stool,
knowing Momma trusts me to learn
a recipe used in my family since
Bubbe's mother came to America on a boat.
So many years ago, no one remembers
quite when or from where.

The meringues come out of the oven
looking crispy but too gooey-warm to eat.

Momma says we should have one anyway.

"I like them best like this," she whispers, as if it's a secret. "Messy."

The kitchen is quiet. Sammy is sleeping upstairs, and Daddy is reading in the den.

For once, Momma is all mine. We lick chocolate off our fingers and smile.

The Seder Table

For us, the Passover Seder is always
in Redmont with Bubbe and Zayde,
aunts, uncles, cousins, and mountains of food.

I love the long tables in the living room,
covered with white linens, where twenty people
can smile at each other, singing Seder songs.

"Dayenu," my favorite, has fifteen verses
and a catchy chorus that goes on and on.

One miracle would have been enough,
the song says, to make us grateful.
And I am, especially when Aunt Risa says
how she loves to sit beside me,
hearing a voice sweet enough
for a record on the radio.

And I am grateful Jenny and Allison
are with us this Passover, not in Philadelphia
with Uncle Morton's parents.

My girl cousins—Jenny, a grade ahead
and Allison, a grade below—have grandparents
in two cities, not just one like me.

Daddy has no brothers or sisters, no nieces or nephews,
no one to say we need to celebrate one year
with them and one year in Redmont.

Daddy's family didn't "make it out,"
I've heard the grown-ups say. No one wants
to explain to kids what that means. Though I think it
has something to do with a man named Hitler
and a war where lots of people died.

One day I will ask Daddy why his parents
are a small grainy picture I've seen once or twice.
But not at the Seder table, when Daddy's patting
Sammy's curly head, looking so happy
to have what he has, not needing anything more.

Back at School

"Where've you been?" Sue Ellen asks
the first morning I'm back from Redmont.

I was only gone two days. We drove home
at nine o'clock at night. Two hours on the road
so Daddy could return to the print shop
and I could be sleepy at school.

"You missed everything!" Lila is breathless,
like she's run to tell me there was a fire.

So much hubbub over a new boy
in Mrs. Bryan's class.

His name is Jack, and his desk
is by the window,
three seats in front of mine.

I can see his short black hair
and his shoulders leaning
over an open book. But not his eyes,

which Sue Ellen says are different
than anyone else's in Colburn.

"Chinese," Sue Ellen explains,
as if I don't understand what it means
to be different too.

Passover Lunch

Everyone's so busy talking
about the new boy, no one notices
my matzah and cream cheese sandwich.

No one holds their nose
to say my hard boiled eggs smell.

No one complains about matzah crumbling,
making a mess on the cafeteria table.

"He's so quiet!"

"Maybe he doesn't speak English."

"His eyes make me uneasy."

I listen, feeling guilty,
knowing that his eyes
could keep everyone else's off me.

The Circle

Three seconds into recess,
Daniel and his crew
circle the new boy.

Stretch the corners of their eyes
with their fingers.

Start chanting.
Cruel, loud words.

I watch from across the asphalt,
my heart beating
so fast it's hard
to breathe.

Last week, it was me in the circle.
Acting like a deer in headlights,
frozen in place by oncoming cars.

But the new boy is not me.

He doesn't stand there
sniffling, like I do.

The new boy finds a hole
on the other side of Jerry.
Lowers his head like a bull
and charges out of that circle.

All the way to the back door
and the safety of the building.

Inside, he can go to the library
or the nurse's office.

Choices I never
considered before.

Difference

"He got away," Lila says.

We stand there with dropped jaws.
We've never seen anyone escape
Daniel Reynold's hateful mouth.
Not like that. Without tears or anger.
Just speed and strength.

Jack's difference is not like mine,
something he can hide until he's asked
where he goes to church. Something
that slips by until he has to
say his last name.

That might be worse than seeing a smile
turn into pinched lips. Or seeing someone
step back after starting off friendly.

He knows how others feel
the moment they see his face.

Another Reason

"Jack must be sad," I say.
"Everyone staring."

Sue Ellen turns her full face to me.

"What's wrong with you? You can't
be nice to him!"

I hold my breath, not wanting to hear
the ugly words she might speak next.

"He's a boy," she says in a sharp voice.
"It will look like a crush."

A girl in fourth grade
should steer clear of boys
if she doesn't want
snickering behind her back.

Not to mention that smoochy sound
Daniel Reynolds makes when

he thinks someone's sweet
on someone else.

"You can't give Daniel another reason
to tease you!" Lila grabs my arm,
sounding like a mother
trying to protect her child.

She means well. And I'm glad
she cares, even though we both
know Daniel has enough reasons
that one more shouldn't matter.

A New Neighbor on Main Street

Daddy comes into the kitchen
that night with a question for Momma.

"Do the drapes need cleaning?"

Momma chuckles as she stirs the peas.
"Since when do you care about the curtains?"

Daddy's quick to explain
that he doesn't mind dusty drapes.
What he wants has to do with
the new business on Main Street,
his new neighbor, two doors down
from Colburn Printing.

"Mr. Kim bought the dry cleaners
from John Jeffers's son," Daddy says,
"just like I bought Colburn Printing
from Bill Winston's widow
ten years ago.

“I remember.” Momma nods.
“Business was slow at first.”

“Mr. Kim is a New American,” Daddy adds.
Like me.”

Momma considers. “It’s a lot of work
to take the drapes down, Ludwig.”

“What about dresses?” Daddy asks.
“Or my suit for Shabbos?”

“Yes,” Momma agrees. “Your suit
could use freshening.”

Momma pulls the chicken from the oven
while Daddy washes his hands in the sink,
and we all sit down to dinner
with the decision my parents have made
to welcome the Kim family to Colburn.

A Secret about Jack

It doesn't all fit together
until after I've cut my chicken
and I'm chewing
to the sound of Daddy's voice
going on about Mr. Kim—
how he has a son my age
at Pine Hill Elementary.

"Did you meet him, Trudie?"
Daddy asks. "His name is Jae-yong.
Started school this week."

I watch Daddy pushing food
onto his fork with his knife,
eating the way he was taught
in Germany, not the American way
with knife down except to cut,
and I wonder if Mr. Kim knows
as little about his son at school
as my parents know about me.

Jae-yong told Mrs. Bryan his name
was Jack. Not that I blame him,
of course. The kids at Pine Hill
think "Trudie Hamburger" is funny
and foreign, from somewhere else.
Imagine what they'd say
about Jae-yong.

I know a secret about the new boy.
A secret I plan to keep.

Daddy's Shop

It smells of ink, just like Daddy's hands,
and it's noisy when the machines in the back
are running full steam. And it's where I go
on Thursdays after I leave piano lessons
with Mrs. Cartwright on Madison Street,
just four blocks from Colburn Printing on Main.

Daddy's shop has a tall wooden counter
I slip behind so I can stand next to him
while he writes Miss Simmons's order
for a hundred copies of her church bulletin.

Daddy does business with everyone
for thirty miles around. If you need
something printed, my daddy—
with his helper, Mr. Barlow—does the job
and delivers it right to your door.

Sometimes we drop off a bundle
on the way home, but not today.
Daddy wants to drop off

something else: his Shabbos suit
at the Kim Family Cleaners.

I follow him down the block
to a store which looks a lot like Daddy's,
at least from the outside. Striped awning
and white lettering on the window.

DRY CLEANERS & TAILORS

Through the glass, I see someone
my size and wonder if Jack
likes to stand beside his father
greeting customers the way I do.

Daddy Has an Idea

Inside, a man with thick dark hair
counts change at the counter.

He seems startled when the bells on the door
jingle, as if this is the first time all day.

Daddy shows Mr. Kim his suit and asks
how long it will take.

"Tomorrow," Mr. Kim promises with a nod.
"Thank you for your business."

Daddy doesn't leave right away. He stays
for a chat while Jack watches from beside
a silver clothes rack. I lift my right hand
in a weak wave. He does the same.
I feel like we're playing Simon Says
until he winks and I giggle.

Daddy and Mr. Kim keep talking,
talking, talking.

"No one is coming," Mr. Kim complains.

"You need to post your prices," Daddy says.
"Offer discounts."

"Advertise?" Mr. Kim's forehead creases.
"Expensive."

"I can help." Daddy's smile spreads across his face.

He always beams when he thinks he has a good idea.

The Plan

Momma says Daddy's idea
is generous. "Printing flyers for free."

Daddy corrects her: "It's a loan.
Mr. Kim will pay when business picks up."

Momma has more questions.
"Two kids delivering?"

That's the part of the plan
Daddy thinks is most brilliant.

Jack and I will be like paperboys,
leaving a rolled-up sheet at every house,
so neighbors know Kim Family Cleaners
just opened on Main Street. A dollar off
if you clip the coupon.

"Will it work?" Momma asks.

"Worth a try," Daddy says.

Johnny Lewis

It takes three afternoons to deliver
the flyers Daddy made for Mr. Kim.

Jack and I climb the steps
of porch after porch, careful not to make
too much noise as we slip papers
under mats and between screen doors.

On the sidewalk, Jack talks about
missing his cousins in Redmont,
where he was born, not China
like Sue Ellen and the other kids think.

"My parents are from Korea," he says
in clear English with no accent at all.
"They worked with relatives in Redmont."

He sighs. "But they wanted their own business,
and everything's cheaper in a small town."

Jack almost makes me glad
I've lived in Colburn all my life
and never had to leave behind
city life or friends from an old school.

"You didn't have Daniel Reynolds there," I say.

"No," Jack tells me. "I had Johnny Lewis."

Johnny Lewis is why
Jack keeps quiet
when kids whisper
loud enough for him to hear,
why he can move so fast,
why he knows where to hide,
why he doesn't expect
to feel safe anywhere.

Names

We are not alone. Mrs. Kim stands
in a green jacket, watching at every corner.
She reminds me of Daddy on Halloween,
making sure no one snatches Lila and me
when we ring doorbells, asking for candy.

She calls Jack "Jae-yong" just like Mr. Kim,
not the American name Jack gave himself
back in Redmont. Jack says she's okay
with a different name at school, as long as
he keeps his Korean one at home.

I'm jealous, knowing I can't
change "Hamburger" and must stay
chopped meat—food grilled over fire.

Magic Books

Back in Mrs. Bryan's room,
Jack sits reading
a library book that matters more
than Mrs. Bryan's math lesson.

She tells him to pay attention
to the blackboard, and he tries
for a few minutes before
his eyes are pulled back down.

I know he's reading the second book
about Jane, Mark, Katharine, and Martha,
who find magic wherever they go.
Jack told me there are more adventures
on Mrs. Nolan's shelves, and he plans
to read them all.

Later, in the lunchroom,
Jack's alone, still filling
himself with words,
too busy reading to see

Daniel at the next table,
stretching his eyes
and pointing Jack's way.

I watch from my place
beside Lila and Sue Ellen,
thinking how I should ask Mrs. Nolan
in the library for one of those books
Jack has—the ones that make
the nasty whispers of this world
disappear like magic.

No!

It's a pretty spring day.
Sun shining on the asphalt
and the grassy patch
where Jack has settled, his nose
still nestled in his library book.

Sue Ellen's got the double Dutch ropes,
and she needs Lila and me
to turn the handles while she jumps.

For a sweet while, I only hear
the sounds of rhymes, ropes,
and Sue Ellen's shoes
skipping on the blacktop.

Then Jack's voice makes us all turn
around. "NO!" he shouts, grabbing his book
from Daniel, who doesn't let go
until pages are torn. "NO!"

I drop the ropes to hurry over
just as Jack shoves Daniel to the ground
and Mr. Rollins, Monday's recess teacher,
charges up to the scene.

He drags both boys off, one on each arm,
not asking what happened or who saw what.

"We didn't see it all," Sue Ellen says,
her blue eyes staring in a steady warning.
"We can't say who's to blame."

But I sure can make a good guess.

The Words Spill

Jack's library book lies ruined,
ripped pages littering the grass.

Someone should show it to Mrs. Nolan.

And it might as well be me,
since it's Monday, and I'll be there
anyway, shelving books while
the rest of my class is singing.

"What's wrong?" Mrs. Nolan asks
when she sees me, tears dripping,
damaged book in my hands.

I didn't mean to tell her everything.

How Daniel stretches his eyes to tease Jack
and mimics my daddy to torment me.

The words spill like the bucket of suds
Sammy tipped in the kitchen last week,
foaming everywhere.

"How long has this been going on?" Mrs. Nolan asks.

She gets a pad of paper and writes it all down,
promising to bring her notes to Mr. Preston,
the principal, this very afternoon.

I mumble "Thank you" because I don't know
what else to say to a grown-up who wants to help
but may end up making things worse.

You'll Pay

The next morning,
when I reach the front steps
of Pine Hill Elementary, Daniel is waiting
with Jerry, Butch, Bobby, and Harold.

Five circle one.
Lila stands nearby, blinking, her head
tilted to catch every word.

"You'll pay." Daniel hisses, his finger
almost poking my nose. The boys behind him
step closer, making Daniel look taller,
like a long mirror in a funhouse.

"Mr. Preston called my father last night,"
he says. "It better not happen again."

"What?" Lila mouths, her lips open
with silent questions I can't answer until
the bell rings and the bullies run to the door.

"Did you tattle?" Lila asks. "To who?"
When I tell her, she grabs my hands.
"This could be bad," she says. "It could
be bad."

And I know she's right.

Against the Rules

Jack is missing from Mrs. Bryan's classroom,
and Sue Ellen thinks that's fair.

"He knocked Daniel to the ground," she says,
acting it out with her pink painted nails.
"That's suspension. Automatic."

"Only if a teacher sees," Lila says. "And most
of the time, they don't."

Lila has it right. How many times
has Daniel swiped the chocolate milk
off my tray in the lunchroom? That has to be
against the rules, and what teacher has
ever stopped him? Was Mr. Rollins
watching Jack on the playground, waiting
for the new boy everybody thinks is from China
to do something wrong?

Sammy in Momma's Sink

I leave school without many answers,
knowing only that Jack will be out two days
and Daniel's dad doesn't like hearing
from the principal that his son
"should be kinder to others."

At home, Momma's busy with Sammy.
He's climbed the counter and plopped
his little self in Momma's sink
to spray water everywhere.
"He's been a handful all day." Momma plunks
my wet brother down on the floor.
"Thank goodness your daddy comes home for
lunch to give me a few minutes break."

"Did Sammy nap?" I ask, knowing
that's her big wish for every afternoon.

"Not long." Momma sighs before
taking Sammy away for dry clothes.

On the way upstairs, she calls down
with a reminder from Daddy.

"Water your new tree before supper.
Daddy says the weather's been dry."

Sprayer

I leave the house
through the basement back door,
where the long hose
is hooked up to a spigot.

Daddy's attached a sprayer to the end,
making it easy to give my baby tree
a shower in place of the rain
which hasn't come in three days.

I drag the heavy green hose
across my back lawn, my eyes
on the grass, not seeing, at first,
two boys with rolls of toilet paper.

Daniel and Jerry, sneaking up
to mummify my tree!

"Go away!" I raise the sprayer and protect
what's mine without thinking twice.

"Get out of my yard!" I holler, my voice
stronger than the sound of flying water.

Daniel and Jerry scamper off
with toilet paper trailing behind.

I giggle like two-year-old Sammy
playing in the sink.

Should I Be Worried?

I'm still giggling
the next morning at school
when I tell Lila and Sue Ellen.

"Did Daniel get soaked?" Lila asks.

"Hope so," I say, covering another
chuckle with my hand.

"Be careful." Sue Ellen shakes her head
in warning. "Daniel could get even."

It's a thought that's crossed my mind,
and if I wasn't so busy being proud
of myself for standing up to Daniel
at last, I might be worried,
might wonder what he will try next
to make me cry.

How Long Will It Last?

Jack comes back on Thursday,
quieter than ever.

But he smiles in the library
on Friday morning, when Mrs. Nolan
gives him a new book to read.

"I've spoken to Daniel," Mrs. Nolan says
quietly to me. "He won't be
bothering any more readers at this school."

She winks. "Not while I'm around."

So Daniel knows he's being watched.
And so far he's been good, just like Sammy
yesterday, who took a long nap and let Momma
have a peaceful lunch with Daddy.

Things are okay, I think,
signing my name
on little lined cards in the library.

How long will that last?

Gather Your Things, Trudie

In the afternoon, Mrs. Bryan shows a filmstrip
called "Incredible Bats," which tells us bats
aren't really blind and eat insects,
like pesky mosquitoes.

With the lights so dim, I want to doze
and probably would if Mrs. Bryan's
machine didn't ding every time
the knob needed turning.

The whole room feels sleepy.

Until the door opens and Mr. Preston
steps inside. He waves Mrs. Bryan
over to whisper and look in my direction.

Bat wings flap across the screen
while Mrs. Bryan hurries
down my aisle, everyone watching.

"Gather your things, Trudie," she says.
"Mr. Preston will explain."

I follow the principal out of the room,
the sound of the filmstrip
dinging in my ears.

Sit Down, Trudie

The principal's forehead is sweaty
beneath his thin, combed-over hair.

He wants to talk in his office,
a place for kids in trouble,
and that shouldn't be me.

I've not done anything . . . except
spray two boys with water
and tell Mrs. Nolan
who really tore Jack's book.

Mr. Preston's voice is soft and low
when he says, "Sit down, Trudie."

I do as I'm told
with my hands in my lap,
still wondering why I'm here.

"There's been an accident," he begins.
"At your home."

"Sammy?" I ask, thinking how he
climbs everywhere and Momma's
always worrying he'll get hurt.

"No." Mr. Preston shakes his head.
"Your father."

How?

My whole body feels cold,
like someone stuck me
in a freezer.

"Daddy? What happened?"

"I don't know all the details."
Mr. Preston pulls on his collar.
"Only that he fell off your roof."

Our roof? How could that be?

To find out more, I have to sit
in an upright chair, along the wall
across from Mrs. Mason's desk,
the place where all kids wait
to be picked up early from school.

The secretary asks me
if I have a sweater, something to

stop my shoulders from shivering
until Lila's mom comes to get me.

I shake my head and tuck my hands
beneath my elbows. Keep my eyes
on the door.

The Story

Mrs. Cummings hugs me against
her plump chest and keeps her arm
tight around me all the way to her car.

She says we'll talk at her house,
in her kitchen, over ginger snaps
warm from the oven.

And she doesn't tell me a thing
until I'm seated at her table
with a plate and a glass of milk.

"No one could have predicted this," she begins.
"They thought Sammy was sleeping."

Not climbing out of his crib. Toddling
to the open window. Pushing out the screen.
Crawling onto the porch roof,
ten feet off the ground.

Daddy was home, eating last night's leftovers for lunch, when Sammy's cry made Momma run upstairs.

"Thank goodness Sammy stayed put while your father ran for the ladder," Mrs. Cummings says.

"We were all so grateful," she says.

Until Daddy's foot slipped.

Not Alone

Mrs. Cummings saw
everything from her house next door.

Daddy scooping a crying Sammy off the roof,
handing him through the window to Momma,
then turning around just a little too quickly.

"He lost his balance," Mrs. Cummings says.
"Plain and simple."

After Lila's mom called the ambulance,
Jerry's mom from across the cul-de-sac
rushed over, offering to watch Sammy
for as long as we need.

"All the neighbors have promised to help."
Mrs. Cummings pats my hand.
"Your family is not alone."

Daddy's Condition

"Eat something, Trudie." Mrs. Cummings
pushes her plate of ginger snaps closer.
"You mother will call the minute she knows."

Dunking cookies into milk
won't keep my mind off Daddy
and what's happening at the hospital,
where Momma is waiting to see
how many broken bones
and why he wasn't conscious
when they lifted him onto the stretcher.

"Don't worry." Mrs. Cummings strokes
my hair. "I'm sure your daddy's woken up by now."

She gives up on the cookies
and takes out a card game.

"Go Fish is always fun," she says in a chirpy voice,
dealing out five cards. "Let's play while we wait."

I sit silent through three hands,
until the front door opens
and Lila bursts in.

"How's your daddy?" she asks, both hands
crossed over her heart.

Everyone Knows

Mrs. Bryan told the whole class
why I left with Mr. Preston.
"Everyone knows and everyone's praying,"
Lila tells me, sitting down for a cookie
and a glass of milk.

"How did he fall?" Lila wants all the details
I don't want to see in my mind again.

Daddy, in the tan pants and white shirt
he always wears to the print shop,
rolling off the roof, landing
with a thud on the ground.

"Later." Mrs. Cummings shushes Lila.
"Now is not the time for that. Not when
we're still waiting on news from the hospital."

So we go back to playing cards. Lila's eyes on the phone.
Mrs. Cummings watching too. Everyone listening
for the ring that will tell us if Daddy woke up.

Answered Prayers

"Hallelujah!" Mrs. Cummings shouts
before handing me her yellow wall phone.
"Our prayers answered."

Momma's voice sounds thin against my ear,
like she just finished a coughing fit. She promises
Daddy will be okay, as soon as he recovers
from a cut, a concussion,
four cracked ribs, and a broken leg.

He'll be staying at Stone Valley Medical a few days.

"Can I talk to him?" I stand by the wall,
holding the phone with both hands.

"Not now," Momma answers. "He needs rest.
A lot of rest."

Sleepover

Momma tells me to give the phone back
to Mrs. Cummings, who moves out of
the room as far as the cord will reach.

I can still hear most everything
on Mrs. Cummings's end.

"Of course Trudie can stay the weekend with us.
You should spend every minute at the hospital."

Lila grabs my hand and squeals.
"Sounds like we're having a sleepover."

"In the den?" I ask, feeling giggly bubbles rise.

Snacks. Board games.
Pillows. Sleeping bags.

We have a routine
we're busy planning

as we check the cupboards for cocoa
to go with popcorn and pretzels.

Last time I spent the night at Lila's
was months ago. Before she went
to the country club party without me,
before she decided we should sit
with Sue Ellen at lunch, walk her home.

And I'm so busy being excited that I forget
for just a moment why it's happening.

Daddy's in the hospital.

He fell off the roof saving Sammy.

Pizza Night

Lila's family does Friday night on the den sofa,
around the television. Mrs. Cummings orders pizza.

No tablecloth or braided challah. No brisket
or noodle kugel. No candles glowing.

We eat on paper plates so Lila's mom has a day off
from dishes. The difference in our houses
hurts to swallow on a night I should have been
hearing Daddy's voice sing Hebrew blessings.

"Is something wrong, Trudie?" Mrs. Cummings asks,
seeing my pizza balanced on my knees, untouched.

Not being hungry, I hadn't noticed right away
the red circles staring up from the gooey cheese.

"Oh, my!" Mrs. Cummings snatches my paper plate.
"I forgot! Jews don't eat pork."

She comes back from the kitchen a minute later
with the pepperoni plucked off.

"There!" she says. "All fixed!"

Mrs. Cummings, so goodhearted,
has never met Rabbi Hertz, who could explain
better why pizza touched by pork
is not exactly fixed for someone Jewish.

But Momma's raised me to always
be polite in other people's houses.
To compliment, not complain.

I thank Mrs. Cummings and eat.

Wear a Clean Dress

The next day, Momma has news
for me over the yellow wall phone
in Mrs. Cummings's kitchen.

Daddy is talking. His head hurts,
but he's eating. A little. His right leg
is wrapped from top to bottom.
He'll come home in a wheelchair
when he gets to come home.

A day no one knows quite yet.

In the meantime, the Braswells
are driving four hours round trip
so Sammy can stay in Redmont
with Bubbe and Zayde
till everything settles down.

Whenever that will be.

The Cummings will take me
to the hospital tomorrow
before church
and pick me up after.

"Wear a clean dress," Momma says,
"and be sure to thank all the neighbors
for being so kind."

Ten or Twelve Weeks

Daddy tries to smile
over his broken leg,
gigantic in a white cast
and raised up on a wire.

He has a bandage on his bald head
where Momma says he got five stitches.

His memory of falling is fuzzy.
Otherwise, he knows names, dates,
and everything else he's supposed to.

"Don't look so sad," he says
in a whispery voice. "The doctors
promise I'll be good as new
in ten or twelve weeks."

Momma lets me sit by the bed
and hold his hand while he rests.

She tells me to remember
something nice. So I pretend
Daddy's hand is squeezing mine
beside the cherry trees in Washington
and I got my wish of never leaving
that happy day.

Broken

Back at Lila's, Mrs. Cummings
says I need clothes for school tomorrow.
She hands me the key to my house,
and I leave out the back door, Lila with me.

We go across the grass from her yard to mine.

"What's wrong, Trudie?" Lila asks as she sees
me hurrying closer to the creek. "What's wrong?"

My cherry tree. It's not
standing, showing off little branches
and leaves. Only a stump is left
with a pointed tip like a sharpened pencil.

Broken. All the way. No hope to get better.
Just like Daddy might have been,
like I was so afraid he was
through all those hours of waiting,
feeling heavy tears behind my eyes,
welling but not falling

until now, when they pour
down my cheeks faster
than I can wipe them away
or blow my nose.

Lila puts her arms around me,
and I soak her shoulder
with sobs so high and loud
they make my body shake.

That Mean

"Who would do this?" Lila asks.
"So mean!"

We stand by the stump of my tree,
looking at each other. There's only one
boy we know who's that mean.

"Daniel was in church this morning,"
Lila says. "So was Jerry."

"They could have done it last night," I say.

Lila tilts her head to the side,
considering. But why?

We can't think of a reason,
not now, with Daddy in the hospital.

"You'd have to be a monster," Lila says.

Which makes me think of a green troll
carrying an axe or a swamp creature
stepping out of the creek with teeth
as long as knives.

Wash Your Face

My head still sore from sobbing,
I turn the key to the house which holds
my clothes right now, but not my family.

Lila thinks my red jumper
with the blue buttons looks nice,
so I pick that for Monday morning,
along with socks and undies,
forgetting I need a blouse too
until Lila reminds me.

"And wash your face," she warns,
"so my mom won't see those tears."

We've decided not to tell grown-ups
about my murdered tree. Lila's mom
would only worry, and Daddy doesn't need
anything else to make him wince.
So for right now, it's my mystery to solve.

If Daniel or Jerry didn't do it, then who
else would? My mind wanders
through a maze, every path
leading to a dark dead end.

Cards and Flowers

My teacher starts the morning
with praise for Daddy.

"Trudie's father is a hero," she says.
"Saving his baby son like that."

Mrs. Bryan asks everyone in class
to practice cursive writing
and make a get-well card I can take
to the hospital next time I go.

No one grumbles, not a word.
Not even Daniel Reynolds.

And the whole day goes like that.

Ginny offers to sharpen my pencil.
George steps aside at the water fountain,
letting me go first. Sue Ellen has cookies
she says her mom made just for me.

At home, there are flowers
from our friends at Beth Israel
and more cards in the mailbox.

I read through every letter,
line by line, and realize
that sometimes
it takes something bad
to find out how good
people can be.

When the Doorbell Rings

At five thirty, Momma is on the phone
with Bubbe, saying that Daddy is better
and she can sleep at home from now on.

When the doorbell rings, Momma's
still busy thanking my grandmother
for keeping Sammy in Redmont
another week. So I'm the one
to open the door and find Jack
on my front steps, holding
a covered dish he brought over
in the basket of his bicycle.

"From my family," he says. "We're all so sorry
about your father's accident."

I take his gift into my arms and stand there
wishing I had something better than
"thank you" to say. Jack felt like a friend
when we delivered flyers a few weeks back,

but not in school, where we could be teased
as boy and girl together.

"What are you reading?" I ask,
and in a snap we're talking about a story
that takes place in the country, with a creek
and a boy who catches frogs. Soon, I'm telling
Jack about the creek in my backyard, which
of course he wants to see.

We leave the covered dish in the kitchen
and go out the back door, waving to Momma
still on the phone.

The Creek

Jack's got his arms out,
balancing, as we step on one stone
after another, following the creek
past the back of Lila's house,
then the McGruders', the Bensons',
and Miss Violet who has
a claw-foot tub in her backyard
filled with mucky water and lily pads.

When we turn back, it's quiet, except for the sound
of a few birds and our sneakers on the stones.
Until Jack's foot slips and splashes us both.
We laugh because the water's cold,
and the creek is shining in the setting sun.

Light lands on the trees beside us,
and Jack stares at something I missed.

Another trunk whittled to a point,
not far from my cherry tree stump,

and a fat, furry creature
with a wide, flat tail.

“Beaver!” Jack screams.

I jump in the air.

Wild Creature

So it wasn't a mean boy or a beast
but a beaver. The news should
make me feel better. No one tried
to hurt me. It just happened.

Like Daddy falling off the roof.

But I don't know how to stop
a wild creature with sharp teeth
waiting to strike again.

"Not easy to control," Daddy said
once to Mr. Pritchard.

They were talking about deer
gobbling roses at night.

Daddy hates it too,
how he can't protect his garden,
how it's so hard to chase away
the things that make us afraid.

Sleep on It

Like me, Jack's never seen
a beaver before. He doesn't know
if they can be scared away or if
they'll eat Daddy's roses
when they've finished chomping
all the trees by the creek.

Jack says I should sleep on it
before I tell Daddy, before
I keep crying over something
that might not happen.

One half of my heart knows
Jack's right. That in the morning
I might not feel gnawed to a nub
like my poor cherry tree.
But the other half of my heart hurts,
thinking about Daddy in the hospital
and wondering what else in my life
could be cut down.

Questions

My feet follow each other,
and the week moves on with Tuesday,
Wednesday, Thursday.

I get up, go to school, eat lunch,
come home. Do math problems.
Read the next chapter in history.
Go to sleep in a silent house
with half my family missing.

Mrs. Bryan asks about Daddy.
The same question every day.
Do I know when
he's leaving the hospital?

No, I don't. But Momma says
he's getting better, little by little,
the way the minutes move on

when I'm sitting at my desk,
circling answers on a worksheet,
wishing every question facing me
was true, false, or multiple choice.

Tree Bark

Even though I'm here on Monday afternoons
when everyone else is in music, I still enjoy
Friday mornings, when Mrs. Nolan
holds up books she recommends
and tells us to take our time choosing.

This Friday, I head straight to the 590s,
the zoology shelf with books
on every animal from *A* to *Z*.
Jack is beside me. He wants to read up
on beavers too. To help me decide
what to do before I tell Daddy
my cherry tree was chewed.

Sitting on the carpet, pages open on our laps,
we learn a full-grown beaver weighs 60 pounds,
builds its home in water, and eats the bark of trees.

Bark but not blossoms? Does that mean
Daddy's roses are safe? I hope.

Though it doesn't send away
my sadness over no pink petals
blooming in my yard next spring.

And it doesn't keep Daniel Reynolds
from seeing Jack and me together
and calling us the perfect couple
for making ugly babies.

"He has those eyes! She has that nose!"
Daniel cackles. "Think what their kids will look like!"

Surprise

Of course I'm not surprised
that Daniel is back to badgering.

It's his nature to cut down,
like a beaver attacking trees.

He's the one surprised
to turn around and find Mrs. Nolan
standing behind him, hands on her hips.

For once, Daniel's been caught
with sharp teeth showing.

His face turns red, blotchy spots
from the neck up, when Mrs. Nolan asks
to speak to him alone in her office.

Jack winks at me
and I wink back.

Invitation

There are more surprises.
Sue Ellen shocks me in the lunchroom.
Between bites of pimento cheese,
she asks if I would like to come
for a sleepover on Saturday night.
Lila is already invited.

I'm not sure how to close
my jaw, considering how
I thought Sue Ellen's family
would never invite someone
to sleep at their house
who couldn't step inside
the Colburn Country Club.

Lila pokes my elbow, urging me
to answer "yes," and I do,
forcing myself to forget

that Sue Ellen was never so nice
before Daddy got hurt and that maybe
I shouldn't be so glad
to be good enough for her now.

At Sue Ellen's

Sue Ellen's house on West Street is tall,
with a long front lawn, white columns in front,
and an American flag waving on a silver pole.

Her bedroom has a canopy bed
with light blue ruffles all around
and a gold cross hanging on the wall.

We admire her dollhouse first,
with its tiny chandeliers and
chairs the size of my pinkie finger.

Lila sighs over six rooms
of itty bitty furniture, wishing
she had something so grand
and pretty. It's the same thought
I'm thinking, though I keep
my sighs to myself.

For dinner, we have macaroni and cheese,
Sue Ellen's favorite and one of mine too.

Then it's back to the bedroom for a night
of painting nails and practicing with makeup
borrowed from Sue Ellen's older sister,
who's away at college and won't know.

There's lots of giggling just before bed
when we wash off red cheeks and blue eyelids
in a bathroom sink, not down the hall, but directly
connected to Sue Ellen's bedroom.

In spite of my doubts, I'm having fun
even when Sue Ellen makes us kneel
by her bed with folded hands.

Of course, I'm not sure what
Rabbi Hertz would say, but I don't mind
when Sue Ellen asks Jesus to bring Daddy
out of the hospital as soon as possible.

After all, that's what I want too.

Mrs. Nolan is Curious

Monday afternoon, I'm humming
in the library while sorting books
from *A* to *Z* for Mrs. Nolan,
who's as pleased as I am to hear
Daddy's coming home Tuesday,
tomorrow, first thing.

"What's that tune?" she asks
through her office door. "So cheerful!"

And being in the smiling mood I am,
I turn my hum to a song just for her.

"What a nice voice you have!"
Mrs. Nolan claps her hands.
"Why don't you sing in school?"

She purses her lips, puzzled
that I've never asked to return
to Mrs. Thompson's class
after Christmas songs ended.

It's not hard to explain.
I didn't feel wanted.

Just like I didn't think
Sue Ellen would ever
invite a Jewish girl
to sleep at her big house.

Was I wrong?

Daddy's Homecoming

Momma was not too hard to convince.

She did need help carrying the flowers
and cards friends sent to cheer Daddy
during so many days in the hospital.

And she agreed my mind would be
on my father, not on my teacher.
I could miss school for one day
to push Daddy's wheelchair
away from that big gray building
with too many floors. Help her get him
settled back home, where he could sip
a chocolate milkshake
in our very own living room.

"Do you need another pillow?"
Momma asks. "Or a sweater?"

I ask about his ice cream treat.
"A second cherry? More whipped cream?"

Daddy laughs and says
he doesn't need pampering.

He's just happy to be home,
even if he does have to sleep
in a rented cot on the first floor
until he learns how to climb
the stairs on crutches.

And I'm just happy to see his face
not bruised anymore from the fall,
and to hear him ask for a song,
the one about the rainbow,
because he wants to drift off
with my voice in his ears.

Crescent Cookies

Lila and her mom come over in the afternoon,
bringing a tin of homemade cookies
Mrs. Cummings made just for Daddy
because she knows how much he likes
her Christmas crescents.

"*Ja!*" Daddy says, powdered sugar on his lips.
"My mother made these for parties
when I was a boy in Berlin."

The crescents are made with nuts and butter.
Mrs. Cummings has been baking them since
she was a little girl. She learned
the recipe from her great-grandma,
who came to this country from Germany too—
two generations ago, long before the war
Daddy doesn't talk much about.
Momma gets iced tea to go along
with the cookies and we visit awhile.
Daddy in the wheelchair, everyone else

on the couch. All of us pleased
to talk about summer, swimming weather,
and how Daddy could be walking by then
with a cane and no cast.

The Note

As she leaves, Lila hands me
homework from Mrs. Bryan.

This gives Momma a reason
to shoo me away from Daddy,
who needs another nap. She says
there's time before dinner
and I should study now.

Upstairs at my desk, I look inside
my history book, the one with questions
to answer after I read Chapter 14,
and find a cream-colored envelope
with my name—*Trudie Hamburger*—
written in Mrs. Bryan's cursive.

Her letters loop and flow across the page,
connecting in a straight and seamless string.

She says she hopes Daddy is resting well. But
there's more under those words, like the loops
beneath lowercase g's and y's.

Mrs. Bryan wants to talk, wants to discuss
Monday music and the library.

Why? Why now? When there are only
six weeks left of school?

When I'm used to things as they are?

Yes, Ma'am

Momma's not as keen
on a second day at home for me.

She says Daddy doesn't need two nurses.

But Daddy does need
someone in the house when she goes
to the supermarket and the pharmacy.

One more day should be all right
with grades as high as mine.
My teacher will understand.

I argue in a voice that doesn't sound
like the Trudie I usually am but a girl
who's speaking out for what she wants.

Momma shakes her head, not so sure,
but admits I've out-talked her this time.

Daddy winks and asks to be wheeled
to the dining room for a jigsaw puzzle.

We're still busy sorting pieces when,
midmorning, Mrs. Bryan calls to check on me.

Momma's out, thank goodness. Not there
to hear Mrs. Bryan ask if everything's all right.

"Yes, ma'am," I say. "We're fine.
And I'll be back tomorrow."

"Good," Mrs. Bryan says. "Did you get my note?"

"Yes, ma'am," I say again, holding the phone tight
against my ear. "I've been thinking about it."

At those words, Daddy's eyes rise from the puzzle,
and he sees the hot blush I'm feeling spread up my neck.
He knows something's wrong.

My daddy is smart that way.

Our Cherry Tree

"Trudie?" Daddy asks, his voice low and gentle.
"Are you keeping something from me?"

I look at his brown eyes, so wide I can see
green flecks inside. And I feel the heat rising
again to my cheeks.

There's more than one secret I'm keeping.
More than one thing I could tell.

So I cry about the cherry tree.
How a beaver chewed it down. How
I'll always treasure our special day
in Washington, even if our souvenir
won't bloom every spring as planned.

"I will always love that tree," I promise,
sobbing in his shoulder.

He holds me for a while. When he pulls me back
to face him, I see his head shaking "no."

"A beaver has teeth," Daddy says. "But
not sharp enough to stop us."

He's a stubborn man, he says,
and will replant. Something he's done
before, in his garden and in his life.

"Don't worry, Trudie," he says.
"We'll have our tree again."

Still the Jewish Girl

After all those tears over the tree,
it would have been nice to forget
my other problems, to turn back
to our jigsaw puzzle. To put the pieces
in place for that pretty picture on the box
of a boat and a bridge and a blue lake
on a sunny day in a city I've never been.

But Daddy isn't satisfied. He wants to know
what else is missing from the puzzle
he heard on the phone with Mrs. Bryan.

"Did you stay home for me or for you?" he asks,
turning the faucet back on, the one that streams
from my eyes any time I'm scared or sad
or just don't know what to do.

"How can this be?" Daddy asks
when I finally tell him. "Your mother thought
the library was only for Christmas."

But nothing changed when December ended.
I was still the Jewish girl who didn't love
the songs everyone else did.

I was still different.

Different

Daddy doesn't like the way I say
that word, "different." Doesn't like
when it pulls people apart,
puts some on a pedestal
and others in the dirt.

"That's what happened in Germany," he says, his voice
growing husky. "Jewish children pushed out of school,
kept out of parks and swimming pools."

Daddy's bald head breaks out in beads of sweat.
The air coming out of his nostrils is suddenly noisy.
Daddy's past is pushing into the present for
the first time I can remember, taking over the Daddy
I know, who's told me a thousand times how
happy he is to live in America, but not once
why he left the country where he was born. Why
he never saw his parents, my grandparents, again.

"You are young, Trudie," Daddy says. "One day, I can explain more. But you can know for now that when I was young, it was dangerous for me to be different, to be a Jew in Germany. My parents sent me away to save my life."

You Are an American

Daddy should understand.
Why it's hard to go back
to Mrs. Thompson's music class
after being asked to leave.

He didn't go back to Germany
after the war that changed
everything.

Daddy still questions me.

He says "hate" starts with separation
and grows bigger, until it turns to stones
angry people throw through windows.

"You are an American," Daddy says.
"You have a right to sing in this country."

Momma's Thoughts

When Momma returns
with a white drug store bag
and groceries for dinner,
Daddy wants to talk to her.

"Something serious," he says.

She puts the milk away
and watches Daddy take his pill
before she sits down with us
in the dining room beside
the unfinished jigsaw puzzle.

Daddy begins, the way I did,
with the easier-to-explain news
about how he'll be buying
a new tree from Mr. Pritchard
to replace the one chopped down.

Momma's face shows worry
over the thought of a beaver

in her backyard. She wants to know
if they bite children and how she
can keep Sammy safe, but calms
quickly at Daddy's promises and
stays that way for the next confession,
which doesn't bother her one bit.

"So what?" Momma shrugs. "This way we
never have this music problem again."

Up to Me

Daddy turns
his wheelchair to the wall.

Momma leaves the room
to unpack the groceries.
Cans of peas and corn.
Clunk! Clunk! Clunk!
On the kitchen counter.

Before this afternoon,
I've seen my parents disagree
with glances, tilted chins,
wrinkled brows. Never words
in front of me.

And never before
have they thrown the decision,
like a towel on a wet floor,
for me to wipe up.

They have decided I will be
the one to tell Mrs. Bryan
what I want to do
about Monday music.

As if I knew my answer.

For Just a Moment

Thursday morning, Momma sends me
out the door in time to walk with Lila,
down the tree-lined street to Pine Hill Elementary
and Mrs. Bryan's question about Monday music.

As we turn out of Bellwood Court, Jerry Braswell
rides up on his bike. He stops to ask how Daddy is
and when Sammy's coming back from Redmont.
At that moment, Jerry is our neighbor again,
the red-haired boy who came out on summer nights
with a jar to catch fireflies, not the boy who snorts
beside Daniel Reynolds in the lunchroom.

When Jerry rides off, we wave
like we could all be friends again.

For a moment, with the spring sun shining
on my face and flowers popping by my feet,
it feels as if all the problems in the world
only need a simple smile to fix. So I tell Lila

what's going on with Monday music
and ask if she knows what I should do.

"Come back!" She grabs my hands.
"We're singing all new songs!"

Some fun and fast, Lila tells me. Some sweet and high,
just like my voice. And there's going to be a concert
at the end of the year. With solos for girls and boys.

"I'm going to audition," she says. "You should too."

Like Everybody Else

I feel turned around,
like I'm wearing a blindfold
in a party game.

I don't know where to pin my hopes.

For so long, I thought singing at school
was for Lila and Sue Ellen, not for me.

Now there seems to be more I could try
than a reading race or a spelling bee.

Lila says Mrs. Thompson will choose
three girls and three boys. Strong voices
needed for a special song.

"If Sue Ellen gets picked, and you, and me . . ."
Lila hops up and down. "We could
practice together in my basement."

I think of all the rainy afternoons we've twirled
on her checkerboard tiles, pretending to be on stage.

And wonder if maybe it's time I tried harder
to belong, to stop worrying about words
and just open my mouth and sing
like everybody else.

I Raise My Hand

When Monday afternoon comes,
I feel tingly walking past the library doors,
down the long hall, and around the corner
to Mrs. Thompson's music room
with the shiny upright piano.

I stand straight, take a deep breath
in front of my metal chair, sing
Mah-May-Me-Mo-Moo and Do-Re-Mi
to warm up my vocal chords
exactly the way I'm told.

After warmups, Mrs. Thompson
asks for names. Who wants to audition?

I picture my piano teacher, Mrs. Cartwright,
clapping in the front row, concert night.
Daddy beside her, beaming.

I raise my hand high.

It Wouldn't Be Fair

"Trudie," Mrs. Thompson calls as the class files
out of the room. "Can we speak a moment?"

I meet her by the upright piano and see
the names for solos on a yellow note pad.

Mine is not there.

"It wouldn't be fair," Mrs. Thompson says.
"Not when you've been absent all these months."

Tears blur my eyes as I turn away.

Daddy was wrong. Some people have
more rights than others.

Mistake

At the end of the line,
in the hallway, going back
to Mrs. Bryan's class,
I pass the library.

Mrs. Nolan is near the door,
waving through the window.
I nod, hoping my eyes
don't look too red.

I don't want her to see
I made a mistake,
leaving her cozy room
for a chance to be a star
somewhere else.

She warned me
when I told her why
I wanted to go back.
She said I didn't need a solo
to sing with my class.

Mrs. Nolan might also say
I don't need to win
Mrs. Bryan's reading race
to enjoy the books
she gives me each week.

Mrs. Nolan doesn't understand
why someone like me
wants stars on a chart
to prove I'm better
than some people think.

Lessons Learned

Sammy greets me when I open the door.
His little legs run on tiny bare feet to tell me
Bubbe's made chocolate chip cookies.

"Chips! Chips!" he shouts
in his one-word talk, chocolate
smeared on his cheek.

I feel my mouth turn up in a smile
despite my disappointing day. Sammy's face
sparkles like glitter, so happy to show me
the cookie crumbling in his balled right fist.

He came home this morning with Bubbe and Zayde
to spread toys all over the house in three seconds flat.

So things are looking more normal,
if not exactly like they were.

Bubbe's here for a few weeks to keep
an eye on Sammy while Momma runs the desk
at the print shop and Daddy rests.

Zayde is going home to Redmont
to sleep in his own bed, but not before
Bubbe sends him upstairs with a hammer
to nail Sammy's window shut.

"Makes me feel safer," she says. "One problem solved."

It's the grown-up way to fix things.
To lock kids out or in,
so they don't try the same thing again.

I don't know if Sammy learned a lesson. But I did.
At least when it comes to Mrs. Thompson.

First Family Meal

We're eating spaghetti.
Sammy's slurping the strings
because I taught him how.

We have a little contest.
Sammy in his high chair
and me in my seat, seeing
who can slurp faster until
Momma makes me stop.

Bubbe shakes her head, happy
to hear giggles after the worries
of last week.

Daddy grins too, proud he used
his crutches to reach the table
and sit upright as if he didn't
have a broken leg at all.

He shows me how to spin my spaghetti
onto a fork, the more grown-up way.

I want to savor every bite.

And I want my cute baby brother
to keep stuffing noodles in his mouth,
laughing like he never was away
and nothing bad ever happened.

Beaver News

As we're clearing the dishes, the phone rings.
Mr. Cummings wants to come by.

"Social call?" Momma asks.

"Not sure," Daddy says, easing himself
back into the wheelchair. "George said
there was something to discuss."

Mr. Cummings strides into our living room,
dressed in a red bowling shirt,
with Lila beside him.

Momma invites us all to sit by the cookies
Bubbe sets on the coffee table. I wait,
as I've been taught, for guests to take first
and smile when Mr. Cummings nods
his approval and thanks.

"Mmm. Chocolate chip."

While he eats, Mr. Cummings gets to business
with news I already know. Two trees on his side
of the creek, cut by beaver teeth. That's three now,
counting my cherry tree.

"The beavers need to be trapped," he says,
"and shipped off to a new home."

"Far away from us," Lila adds, biting a cookie.

"Mr. Pritchard at the nursery knows a man,"
Mr. Cummings says. "He'll give us a fair price."

"I'll pay my share," Daddy promises from his wheelchair.

"Wait till you're back on your feet," Mr. Cummings says,
rising from the couch to shake Daddy's hand
and mention news I haven't heard before.

"Money must be tight right now."

Good Neighbors

Before Mr. Cummings leaves for his bowling league
and Lila goes home to bed, we talk about
my missing cherry tree. Mr. Cummings says
Lila told him how I cried to find it cut down,
and there's no need to wait
till Daddy's out of the wheelchair.
"I can help," he says.

"And I can too," Lila chimes in.
"We want Trudie to have her tree again."

When the door closes, Daddy turns to me,
his brown eyes misty.

"In my life," he says, pulling a handkerchief
from his pocket, "I've seen people turn their backs
when others suffer."

"But today," he says, "true neighbors show me
the best of what people can be."

That's twice in one week
I've heard Daddy bring up the past.
He wants me to understand I can't trust
all people to be good, but not everyone is bad.

"The world has both," he says,
wiping his eyes. "Both."

Switching Places

In the morning, Momma's wearing
a perky yellow print at breakfast. She'll leave
the house instead of Daddy to help Mr. Barlow
at Colburn Printing, where Daddy wishes he was.

Ten times a day, Daddy rolls his wheelchair
to the phone so he can check on the shop
with Mr. Barlow, who's doing the best
he can on his own. But it's hard to run
the machines and the front desk
at the same time.

Not to mention deliveries.

Business is suffering. Daddy is sighing.

But Momma's face is as perky as her yellow dress.
She picks up her purse and kisses everybody's
head, including Daddy's, on the way out the door.

The color in her cheeks makes me wonder
if Momma's quite as sad as Daddy
over switching places. If she might like
greeting customers and taking orders at the shop
just as much as he does.

Bubbe's Love

Once Momma is out of the house,
it's my turn to leave. Bubbe checks
to make sure my dress is clean
and turned right-side out. Somehow,
she hasn't forgotten the time in first grade
I wore my jumper backwards.

"I'm not treating you like a baby, Trudie,"
she says when I fuss. "Just helping you
look your best on this big day."

That makes my pout puff into a smile.
I'm enjoying eyes on me, for a change,
in this house where Sammy needs
so much watching
and Daddy still needs nursing.

"I'm proud," Bubbe says as she pecks
my cheek, "of my superstar reader."

She follows me to the porch,
her hand in a wave, until I'm on my way
without falling down the steps
or skinning my knee.

Straight Ahead

Marching past the library and down the hall,
I keep my eyes straight ahead, ready to glide
into Mrs. Bryan's class and feel
forty-nine gold stars shining behind me.

The sky-blue reading race chart
hangs to the left of the door, going out,
not going in. I can't turn and gawk, not yet,
not now, before my fiftieth star is pasted on.

Stopping at Mrs. Bryan's desk,
I open my schoolbag and pull out
the lined paper with my report
on *The Borrowers* by Mary Norton,
a book Jack said I might like to read
if I took a break from biographies,
about a family of tiny people
living under the floorboards, using thimbles
for pails and empty spools for seats.

Mrs. Bryan winks as she takes my paper.
"Looks like we need a party this Friday."

Once I'm in my seat, my eyes stray to the left
just a little, then back. I want to keep looking ahead
until I've made it all the way to my goal.

Fifty Stars

By lunchtime, there are fifty stars
on the reading race poster, same number
as the stars on the flag outside the school.

Everyone knows there will be a party
on Friday with donuts and juice.

My heart is on a flagpole too, flying so high
I don't feel teased when Jerry asks
if my eyes are tired from so much reading.

I tell myself he's honestly asking—concerned,
like any good neighbor, about my health.

And I don't feel shy when Jack steps
near to ask if I liked *The Borrowers*
and if I'm planning to read
the others Mary Norton wrote.

"Absolutely," I say in a voice loud enough
for anyone to hear, anyone to see
Jack is my friend, someone who doesn't
doubt, not for a second, that I deserve
the chance to call myself a winner.

Not the Time

At home, I can't stop talking
about the reading trophy
and the party on Friday.

I want to pick my dress now,
to be sure I'll look special.

Bubbe says we should go shopping.
Buy a new one.

"A spring print with a collar
and a sash," Bubbe says.

Momma tightens her lips
and says, "No. This is not
the time for this family
to be spending money."

Bubbe covers her mouth
with her hand, like someone
who knows she's made a mistake.

In a silent room, two grown-ups
eye each other with words I know
won't be spoken in front of me.

Gold

Bubbe has another idea
to make Friday special.
Something even better
than a new dress. Jewelry!

"Gold brightens up any outfit,"
Bubbe says. "You could wear
my pendant for just one day."

Bubbe pats a rose on her chest.
The gold rose she's worn every day
I can remember, the necklace
from Zayde that matches her name.

"Let's see how it looks," Bubbe says,
hanging her rose around my neck.

We stand together at the mirror.

Some of the girls at school, including Lila
and Sue Ellen, wear crosses on gold chains.

Bubbe's right. A little gold
can make a plain blouse sparkle.

Except Bubbe's rose is lots bigger
than Sue Ellen's cross and droops
down my front, flopping this way and that.

"It's too big," Momma declares. "For a little girl."

But Momma has just the thing—
a treasure she's kept in her jewelry box
from when she was ten, like me,
and Zayde gave her a gift she wore
every day, under her dress, for years.

"Your Jewish star!" Bubbe touches
Momma's shoulder.

"Time to hand it down," Momma says.
"Mother to daughter. A tradition begun!"

Jewish Star

Two tiny triangles
intertwined
inside a circle
with six gold points.
A delicate design
my fingers touch
lovingly, as mine.

"No need to show it off
at school," Momma whispers
by my cheek.

"Keep it special against your heart,"
she says. "A private reminder
of who you are and what
you believe in."

Secrets

All day Thursday, in Mrs. Bryan's class,
I feel the warm wiggle of my star
beneath my blouse. No one knows it's there
except me. Though I'm dying to show Lila
I have a necklace, pretty as the cross
she wears, and fourteen-karat gold.

Social studies, math, lunch, English.
The day goes fast. Soon, I'm walking
to Mrs. Cartwright's with my piano books,
hoping she'll forgive me for not going
to the basement more than once this week
to practice on the old blonde upright
Daddy likes to brag he bought for a song.

I don't show Mrs. Cartwright my star either,
remembering the angel she gave me
for the Christmas tree I've never had.

The angel lies tucked in a drawer
behind my barrettes. Another secret
I haven't shared.

Like Always—Almost

After piano, I walk to the shop
like always. Except it isn't like always.
Momma is behind the counter,
talking to Miss Johnson
about invitations to her wedding.

They are picking paper, envelopes,
and letters with curlicues.

"Do you want a satin ribbon
for an extra touch?" Momma points
to a sample in a giant book.

Her smile is something I expected.
Momma steps out in the mornings
so quickly now. I know
a day at Colburn Printing
is no chore for her.

But there is something I don't expect.

A wheelchair in the back room
with Mr. Barlow, who's watching
papers shoot out of machines.

Tired of secondhand news, Daddy's come
to check on his business in person.

It feels right to see him here
on a Thursday, like always.

If only he was standing up
and walking around
like always.

Deliveries

Daddy's business
is on Main Street, only a mile
from our house—walkable for me
but not for a man in a wheelchair.

I don't have any idea how Daddy
made it to the shop until Mr. Kim
comes by with Jack at closing time.

"Do you need another ride?"
Jack's dad asks. "My van is ready."

"No need," Daddy says. Momma can put
the wheelchair in the station wagon,
and he's okay for short stretches on crutches.

"Besides," Daddy says, "you've done enough
with deliveries. We're so grateful."

That's when I find out Mr. Kim has carried
more than my father in his van this afternoon.

"I'm out with my own business," he says. "No trouble
to make a few extra stops."

Mr. Kim's been dropping off Daddy's orders
along with dry cleaning, delivering
true friendship in our time of need.

My Name

While the grownups keep chatting,
Jack takes me aside. He has news,
he says, that will make me happy.

"I saw Mrs. Bryan on Main Street today.
Coming out of Mr. Gordon's store."

"The jewelry shop?" I ask, confused.

"Your trophy!" He claps, excited
for me. "It's been engraved."

On the street, Mrs. Bryan,
tickled with how nice it came out,
showed Jack the little plate
at the bottom of my trophy.

"It said *Trudie Hamburger: Top Reader*
in big block letters."

My name on a trophy!
That's even bigger than bringing home
a cup with two fancy handles, each curved
like one half of a heart.

My name. Trudie Hamburger,
engraved in gold for all to see.

The Last Word

My trophy sits
on Mrs. Bryan's round table
in the back, surrounded by donuts
and paper cups filled with juice.

It looks taller with my name
printed on the bottom.

Mrs. Bryan asks the whole class
to raise their cups in a toast to me.

I can feel myself grinning,
a smile that glows inside me all day,
even on the playground when Daniel
says he couldn't bear to have a name
like mine on a trophy.

"It means meat!" he cackles. "Chopped meat.
Something a butcher grinds up."

"Something people cook on the fourth of July,"
I answer. "An all-American food!"
Daniel blinks as if he can't believe
someone like me, with a dad from somewhere else,
knows what Americans eat. But he doesn't say more
because I got the last word today.

My name is Hamburger. An all-American food.

Not the Only One

Before the recess whistle blows,
I do one more thing I wish I'd done
the first time I had the chance.

I pull the gold chain out
from under my collar
and show Lila and Sue Ellen
my star, the one Momma saved
to give to me and I will save
for a daughter of my own.

"Pretty!" Lila coos until
Sue Ellen butts in to tell us
that her cross came from
her great-granny. So I'm not
the only one with a family tradition.

She tosses a curl as she says it,
reminding me I'm still the same Trudie
not allowed in Colburn Country Club.

Except the truth she's said doesn't change.

I'm not the only one. My family has traditions
just like everyone else. I'm different,
but not in every way.

A New Tree

Three Sundays later,
I'm in my backyard with Lila and Jack,
pushing my shoe against a shovel,
listening to Daddy on his crutches
telling us how deep the hole should be
for the baby tree Mr. Pritchard
brought wrapped in a burlap diaper.

"Good thing it rained last night," Daddy says.
"The ground is softer."

"And muddier!" Jack laughs, pointing at his shoes.

Lila laughs with him, lifting her sneaker.

I don't know if Lila meant to make friends
with Jack, but she doesn't seem to mind
how often he comes by to play tag
or throw stones into the creek.

We were both glad to see him
show up this afternoon,
as we were pushing pointed blades
into the grass, wondering if we'd made
too big a promise to Daddy
about having the strength
to dig as deep as needed.

Jack picked up a shovel
without even being asked
and he's been right here
since, smiling beside us,
helping to mix peat moss
and place a new tree gently
into a hole three friends made
together, taking turns.

By Next Spring

After the tree is snug in the ground,
Mr. Cummings comes over
with some wire mesh to circle
the trunk, just in case Mr. Beaver
has more friends than we know.

"Or if Mr. Deer comes by," Daddy adds.
"I should have put up a fence the first time."

Mr. Cummings chuckles. "You can't change the past."

"That's right," Daddy agrees. "Only the future."

We all walk around the wire fence, touching it,
testing its strength. Lila, Jack, Mr. Cummings.
Daddy too. He's out of the wheelchair
for good now, using only crutches.

It won't be that much longer, the doctor says,
before Daddy will be out of the cast, using a cane.

Mama says by next spring, Daddy's accident
will be a memory, behind us.

By next spring, my tree will be taller. I should be too.

But right now, I'm looking at Lila and Jack,
playing tag, calling my name. And I'm happy
to be running toward them, right into the future.

About the Author

Jacqueline Jules is the author of fifty books for young readers including the Zapato Power series, the Sofia Martinez series, *The Hardest Word, Picnic at Camp Shalom, Light the Menorah: A Hanukkah Handbook, Sarah Laughs, Never Say a Mean Word Again*, and *Tag Your Dreams: Poems of Play and Persistence*. She grew up in southern Virginia. Visit her at www.jacquelinejules.com.